Woodland Christmas

Woodland Christmas

Twelve Days of Christmas in the North Woods

by

FRANCES TYRRELL

SCHOLASTIC INC.

New York Toronto London Auckland Sydney
Mexico City New Delhi Hong Kong

**The illustrations for this book were done
in watercolor on Arches rag paper.**

ISBN 0-590-86368-1

16 15 14 13 12 11 10 9 8 7 6 5   0 1 2 3 4 5/0

Printed in the U.S.A.   09

First Scholastic Trade paperback printing, November 2000

Typeset in Galliard

The animals in this book are:
one gray partridge,
two rock doves, three ruffed grouse,
four common loons, five river otters,
six Canada geese, seven whistling swans, eight raccoons,
nine red foxes, ten moose, eleven red squirrels,
and twelve beavers.
The bird in the potted pear tree
is a California partridge,
and the courting couple are black bears.

On the first day of Christmas,
My true love gave to me
A partridge in a pear tree.

On the second day of Christmas,
My true love gave to me:
Two turtledoves
And a partridge in a pear tree.

On the third day of Christmas,
My true love gave to me:
Three French hens
Two turtledoves
And a partridge in a pear tree.

On the fourth day of Christmas,
My true love gave to me:
Four calling birds
Three French hens
Two turtledoves
And a partridge in a pear tree.

On the fifth day of Christmas,
My true love gave to me:
Five golden rings
Four calling birds
Three French hens
Two turtledoves
And a partridge in a pear tree.

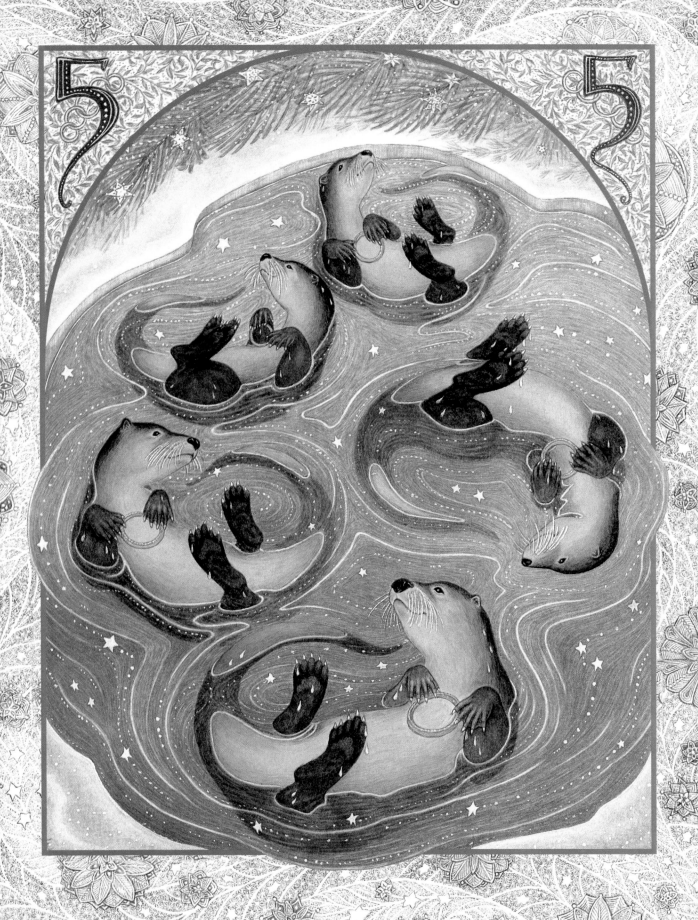

On the sixth day of Christmas,
My true love gave to me:
Six geese a-laying
Five golden rings
Four calling birds
Three French hens
Two turtledoves
And a partridge in a pear tree.

On the seventh day of Christmas,
My true love gave to me:
Seven swans a-swimming
Six geese a-laying
Five golden rings
Four calling birds
Three French hens
Two turtledoves
And a partridge in a pear tree.

On the eighth day of Christmas,
My true love gave to me:
Eight maids a-milking
Seven swans a-swimming
Six geese a-laying
Five golden rings
Four calling birds
Three French hens
Two turtledoves
And a partridge in a pear tree.

On the ninth day of Christmas,
My true love gave to me:
Nine ladies dancing
Eight maids a-milking
Seven swans a-swimming
Six geese a-laying
Five golden rings
Four calling birds
Three French hens
Two turtledoves
And a partridge in a pear tree.

On the tenth day of Christmas,
My true love gave to me:
Ten lords a-leaping
Nine ladies dancing
Eight maids a-milking
Seven swans a-swimming
Six geese a-laying
Five golden rings
Four calling birds
Three French hens
Two turtledoves
And a partridge in a pear tree.

On the eleventh day of Christmas,
My true love gave to me:
Eleven pipers piping
Ten lords a-leaping
Nine ladies dancing
Eight maids a-milking
Seven swans a-swimming
Six geese a-laying
Five golden rings
Four calling birds
Three French hens
Two turtledoves
And a partridge in a pear tree.

On the twelfth day of Christmas,
My true love gave to me:
Twelve drummers drumming
Eleven pipers piping
Ten lords a-leaping
Nine ladies dancing
Eight maids a-milking
Seven swans a-swimming
Six geese a-laying
Five golden rings
Four calling birds
Three French hens
Two turtledoves
And a partridge in a pear tree.

The Twelve Days of Christmas

Moderately F · · · C7 · F · F · B♭ · F · C7

On the first day of Christ - mas my true love gave to me A par - tridge _ in a pear

F · % F · · C7 · F · C7 **(Repeat as needed)**

tree. 2. On the sec-ond
3. On the third day of Christ - mas my true love gave to me two tur-tle-doves,
4. On the fourth three French hens. } And a
four call-ing birds,

F · B♭ · F · C7 · F · **D.S.** · F · · C7 · F

par - tridge _ in a pear tree. 5. On the fifth day of Christ - mas my true love gave to me

F · G7 · C · · C7 · F · GM

five gold - en rings, four _ call-ing birds, three French _ hens,

C7 · F · B♭ · F · C7 · F · % · F

two _ tur-tle-doves, And a par - tridge _ in a pear tree. 6. On the sixth
7. On the sev-enth
8. On the eighth
9. On the ninth day of Christ - mas my
10. On the tenth
11. On the elev-enth
12. On the twelfth

C7 · F · C7 · F · G7 · C

true love gave to me Six geese a - lay - ing five gold-en rings,
Sev-en swans a - swim-ming
Eight maids a - milk-ing
Nine la - dies danc-ing
Ten lords a - leap-ing
Elev-en pip-ers pip-ing
Twelve drum-mers drum-ming

C7 · F · Gm · C7 · F · B♭ · F · C7 · F · **D.S.**

four _ call-ing birds, three French hens, two _ tur-tle-doves, And a par - tridge _ in a pear tree.